# The Mystery of the Lost Island

# THREE COUSINS DETECTIVE CLUB®

---

9703

# The Mystery of the Lost Island

Elspeth Campbell Murphy

Illustrated by Joe Nordstrom

**BETHANY HOUSE PUBLISHERS**
MINNEAPOLIS, MINNESOTA 55438

*The Mystery of the Lost Island*
Copyright © 1997
Elspeth Campbell Murphy

Cover and story illustrations by Joe Nordstrom

THREE COUSINS DETECTIVE CLUB® and TCDC® are
registered trademarks of Elspeth Campbell Murphy.

Unless otherwise identified, Scripture quotations are from the
*International Children's Bible, New Century Version,* copyright © 1986,
1988 by Word Publishing, Dallas, Texas 75039. Used by permission.

Published by Bethany House Publishers
A Ministry of Bethany Fellowship, Inc.
11300 Hampshire Avenue South
Minneapolis, Minnesota 55438

Printed in the United States of America.

**Library of Congress Cataloging-in-Publication Data**

Murphy, Elspeth Campbell.
  The mystery of the lost island / by Elspeth Campbell Murphy.
      p.   cm. — (The Three Cousins Detective Club ; #18)
  Summary: While visiting Lake Misty Pines, the three cousins
hear about an archaeological treasure that may lie on the island in
the middle of the lake and try to track a mysterious stranger.
  ISBN 1–55661–856–5 (pbk.)
  [1. Islands—Fiction. 2. Cousins—Fiction. 3. Mystery and
detective stories.] I. Title. II. Series: Murphy, Elspeth
Campbell. Three Cousins Detective Club ; 18.
PZ7.M95316Mydc      1997
[Fic]—dc21                                        97–21123
                                                      CIP
                                                       AC

ELSPETH CAMPBELL MURPHY has been a familiar name in Christian publishing for over fifteen years, with more than seventy-five books to her credit and sales reaching five million worldwide. She is the author of the best-selling series *David and I Talk to God* and *The Kids From Apple Street Church*, as well as the 1990 Gold Medallion winner *Do You See Me, God?* A graduate of Trinity College and Moody Bible Institute, Elspeth and her husband, Mike, make their home in Chicago, where she writes full time.

# Contents

*"The Lord has made both these things:*
*Ears that can hear and eyes that can see."*

Proverbs 20:12

# 1

## *The Indian Maiden*

$S$arah-Jane was alone the first time she saw the Indian Maiden running through the mist.

Later, when she told her cousins Timothy Dawson and Titus McKay what she had seen, they just looked at her.

Sarah-Jane had seen that look before. It meant: "Our cousin has lost her mind."

But the boys didn't say anything. And Sarah-Jane knew why not.

The three cousins had a detective club. And their detective club had rules.

One rule was that you had to tell the truth. You couldn't lie and say you had seen something odd or mysterious if you hadn't.

The next rule was a little more complicated. It said that the listening cousins had to believe that the talking cousin was telling the truth. But they didn't exactly have to believe the *story* was true. That's because things are not always what they seem. And people can be mistaken.

"You think I'm mistaken, don't you?" demanded Sarah-Jane.

Timothy and Titus just shrugged.

That was another rule. The listening cousins couldn't make fun of what the talking cousin said—no matter how crazy it sounded. It was something like: If you can't say anything nice, don't say anything at all. Besides, the cousins had been around mysteries long enough to know that sometimes the craziest-sounding stuff turned out to be true.

But still.

The Indian Maiden?

Come on.

Sarah-Jane could tell by the looks on her cousins' faces that this was what they were thinking.

And, to be honest, she couldn't really blame them.

Sarah-Jane was known for her vivid imagination. She loved stories—she even wanted to be a writer someday. And the legend of the Indian Maiden was one of her *favorite* stories.

Then, too, it had been foggy. It was often foggy at Misty Pines. And the fog could play tricks with your mind. Make you think you were seeing things . . .

Sarah-Jane had just about convinced herself she had imagined the whole thing.

But the second time Sarah-Jane saw the Indian Maiden, Timothy and Titus saw her, too.

# 2

## An Optical Illusion?

*I*t was only a glimpse at a distance. Just enough to see the Indian Maiden disappear into the foggy woods.

But it was enough to be sure that they had seen her. That they had seen *something*, anyway.

"Yo!" said Titus when he could catch his breath. "You weren't kidding, S-J!"

"Of course not," said Sarah-Jane in her most dignified voice. "I never kid."

"Yeah, right," said Timothy. "But at least now we know you weren't just letting your imagination run away with you."

"Of course not," said Sarah-Jane. "I never—"

"Yeah, right," said Titus. "But the point

is—we couldn't *all* be imagining the same thing at the same time!" He paused and thought about this. "*Could* we?"

"I doubt it," said Timothy. "But—what do they call it when your eyes kind of play tricks on you? When you *think* you're seeing something, but you're really not?"

"An 'optical illusion,' " said Sarah-Jane.

"Right!" said Timothy. "Maybe the Indian Maiden was an optical illusion. Maybe we thought we saw her. But it was really something else."

"It couldn't have been *the* Indian Maiden," said Titus. "It *couldn't* have been. I mean, she's just a legend. A story people made up a long time ago."

Sarah-Jane didn't reply. For one wild moment that's *exactly* what she thought she had seen. A legend come to life.

But Sarah-Jane knew that things are not always what they seem. People were always saying, "I couldn't believe my eyes!" Well, sometimes your eyes *did* play tricks on you. And people were always saying, "I couldn't believe my ears!" Well, sometimes you *shouldn't* believe everything you hear.

But Sarah-Jane also knew that you had to use your eyes and ears wisely to find things out.

The story-loving part of her wanted to leave things as they were.

She wanted to believe that she had seen the beautiful Indian Maiden from the Misty Pines legend. Really, truly seen her. But from a nice, safe distance. It would be a good story to tell her grandchildren someday.

But the detective part of Sarah-Jane knew that she had to get to the bottom of things.

"Gentlemen," she said to her cousins. "We need to take a closer look."

# 3

# *Island in the Mist*

$S$o the three detective cousins set off along the footpath that ran beside the shore of Lake Misty Pines.

They had to walk single file, being careful not to trip over tree roots.

This made it hard to talk. But that was all right. They were each lost in thought anyway. They were headed to the spot where they had seen the Indian Maiden appear. Then *disappear*. Who knew what they would find now?

On their left, the water lapped gently against the shore. Sarah-Jane looked across the water to where she could see the outline of an island in the mist.

Sarah-Jane knew the island was farther away than it looked. It was hard to tell

distances over water—which was still another way your eyes could play tricks on you!

The island's real name was Gull Island. But Sarah-Jane never thought of it by that name. It's not that she had anything against sea gulls. Just the opposite. They were almost her favorite bird. But an island so shrouded in fog needed a better, more mysterious name. So to herself and her cousins Sarah-Jane called it Lost Island.

And there was another reason this was a good name. It was because of the story.

Long, long ago at the beginning of time, there lived a peaceful Indian tribe on the shores of Lake Misty Pines. The tribe had been entrusted with a special treasure. (The story was never clear about just what that was.) One day scouts brought back news that enemy warriors were coming.

The Indian Maiden who lived in the sky took pity on the peaceful people.

She came down from the sky on a magical canoe and carried the villagers and their treasure to safety on the island. Then she dipped the hem of her long skirts into the lake and rose up into the air. She wrung out the water, and this water filled the air as fog—which completely hid the island from view.

When the enemy arrived, they found the village deserted. Where could the villagers have gone? they wondered. The canoes were still pulled up on shore. The enemy warriors never even saw the island. The mystery of the missing villagers frightened them so much that they left and never came back.

The grateful villagers returned to their homes. But they left their treasure on the island, where to this day, the Indian Maiden guards it with fog.

And it was said that on foggy days you could still catch a glimpse of her running through the mist or gliding across the lake in her magic canoe.

But the treasure—if ever there was a treasure—remained lost to the world.

# 4

## A Startling Discovery

*T*he island wasn't always covered by fog, of course. On bright, sunny days it was an ideal spot for a picnic.

No one lived on the island. It was a wildlife preserve—a place set apart for animals and birds. But people could visit for the day. They could even get a permit to camp overnight. (Except that this year the island had been closed to the public before the end of the season. Something to do with some scientific work that was going to go on there.)

During the regular summer season, there was a small ferryboat. It operated from the town at the end of the lake, taking visitors back and forth to Gull Island—or Lost Island, as Sarah-Jane called it.

Sarah-Jane loved the island, and she loved the ferryboat. She had been on the ferryboat lots of times. But it was her first trip that the family still told about. It was one of those instant family legends.

Sarah-Jane had been quite small when she and her parents first started coming to Misty Pines.

That first year, her parents had wanted to prepare her for a new experience. So they had told her they were all going to the island on a ferryboat.

But little Sarah-Jane had thought that they were going to ride a *fairy* boat. And she had looked forward to it with all her heart.

She had burst into tears when she saw that the boat was run by ordinary people.

Her parents hadn't known what was wrong. At first they thought she was afraid of the water. It had taken a while—quite a while—for them to realize that Sarah-Jane was crying because there were no fairies at Misty Pines.

Sarah-Jane smiled to herself. She thought: *I've come a long way, haven't I? I'm not a little kid who expects to see fairies. I'm a big kid who thinks she sees the Indian Maiden.*

To the right of the path lay the woods. And just beyond the woods lay the clearing with the cabins and lodge of Misty Pines Campgrounds. Though the cousins couldn't see the buildings, they knew they weren't far away. And they could hear the ring of hammers.

Sarah-Jane's parents and some other volunteers were doing end-of-the-season repair work.

This meant that there weren't a lot of people around, and the cousins were pretty much on their own. But that was all right. They could handle it. Still, as she walked in the lead along the footpath, Sarah-Jane was glad to know that sensible grown-ups were only a short dash away.

Especially when she almost stumbled over a canoe.

# 5

## A Logical Explanation?

Sarah-Jane stopped dead in her tracks, and Timothy and Titus slammed into her. The boys looked where she was pointing. As detectives, they had trained themselves not to make noise—even when they were surprised.

It would have been easy to pass right by the canoe without seeing it. It was pulled up out of the water and hidden in some bushes.

The first thought that flitted through Sarah-Jane's mind was that she had been right after all. They had seen the Indian Maiden, and here was her magical canoe.

But almost at the same moment she knew her imagination was running away with her again. She saw that it wasn't a magical canoe. It wasn't even an old-time birchbark canoe. It was made of aluminum, sleek and modern. But what was it doing there?

"What is it doing there?" whispered Titus, taking the words right out of her mouth.

"Yes," said Timothy, also keeping his voice down. "I thought no one was here this week except the work crew. And they're too busy to go canoeing."

"Then, who did we see running away from here?" asked Titus.

"Not the magical Indian Maiden. That's for sure," said Sarah-Jane.

"Not unless magical Indian Maidens wear sneakers," agreed Timothy.

Sarah-Jane and Titus looked where Timothy was pointing. There were footprints on the damp path. And they had definitely *not* been made by moccasins—either real or imaginary.

The cousins traced the footprints from the canoe, across the path, and right up to the edge of the woods. Then they lost them.

"That must be what happened when she seemed to disappear," said Sarah-Jane, still speaking softly. "She was only on the path for a little bit. That was when we saw her. Then she was hidden by the woods."

Titus had a new thought. "Do you think she saw *us*?"

"I don't think so," said Sarah-Jane. "She wasn't looking our way."

"Yes," said Timothy. "And I have a feeling she didn't *want* to be seen. The way she hid the canoe. The way she didn't stay on the path."

"I don't think she wanted to be *heard*, either," said Titus. "I mean, aren't canoes the quietest kind of boat there is?"

The cousins looked at one another. They

were all thinking the same thing. They had come looking for a logical explanation and found another mystery. A mysterious stranger at Misty Pines.

"I think we'd better tell somebody about this," said Timothy.

So they slipped off to get Sarah-Jane's parents—moving quickly and quietly, a little bit like canoes themselves.

As they went along, Sarah-Jane's mind made up a little rhyme: *I know what we've seen. But what does it* mean?

She was glad her parents were coming back to see.

But when the cousins got back with the grown-ups, the path had been wiped clean of footprints. And the canoe was gone.

# 6

## A Baffling Situation

*I*t was a baffling situation. All Sarah-Jane could do was sputter. And she didn't even bother to keep her voice down. "But—but—but—but—but—"

"Honey," said her father. "You sound like an outboard motor. Now, just settle down and tell us what's going on."

"But that's just it!" cried Sarah-Jane. "We don't *know* what's going on. All we know is that there was a canoe. Right there! And now it's gone!" She turned to her cousins. "Right?"

Timothy and Titus were nodding so hard they looked like two little bobbing-head toys in a car window.

"I'm sure there's a logical explanation," said her mother soothingly.

"Really?" asked Sarah-Jane hopefully. Maybe they would get to the bottom of things after all. "Like what?"

"Um—well," said her mother. "I don't know right off hand. . . . But I'm sure there *is* one. Anyway," she added briskly. "I think maybe you kids have been on your own too much. How about a trip into town? We'll have lunch and go to the Indian Trails souvenir shop. How does that sound?"

The cousins glanced at one another. Did the grown-ups believe them or not? Sometimes it was hard to tell. Still, lunch sounded like a good idea. Lunch always sounded like a good idea. And the souvenir shop *was* one of their favorite spots on the planet. . . .

Sarah-Jane's father said, "You guys go ahead. I've got stuff to finish up here. And I'll ask around about any strangers anyone might have seen."

The cousins glanced at one another again. Maybe the grown-ups *did* believe them about the "Indian Maiden" and her canoe. Well, it was a baffling situation. And, as detectives, they knew that when you had a baffling situation, sometimes the best thing to do was to take a little break from it. Then you could come back to it later. They agreed on the trip into town.

Sarah-Jane's father took out his wallet and surprised them with some extra money for the souvenir shop.

Then he took out a picture of Sarah-Jane and himself and her mother. He handed the picture to Sarah-Jane and said solemnly, "I want you to have this picture to remember me by. Because by the time you come out of the souvenir shop, you'll be all grown-up. And I will be an old, old man."

Sarah-Jane tried to groan and roll her eyes. But she couldn't help laughing.

It was true. Every year, she and Timothy and Titus would save their money for a trip to Indian Trails. Every year they would spend *hours* roaming up and down the aisles. Looking at all the wonderful fiddly little *stuff*. Trying to *decide*.

Sarah-Jane told her father he'd better keep the picture to remember *her* by.

She felt quite happy as she raced Timothy and Titus to the car.

Sarah-Jane was sure she could just put the mysterious stranger and the disappearing canoe out of her mind.

She was wrong, of course.

# 7

# Indian Trails

"*E*X-cellent!" declared Titus.

"Neat-O!" agreed Timothy.

"So cool!" sighed Sarah-Jane.

They stood just inside the door of the Indian Trails souvenir shop, wondering where to begin.

The store was bigger than last year. It got bigger every year. They had even added some more expensive grown-up stuff.

Sarah-Jane's mother went off to look at some hand-painted pottery that she thought would make a nice wedding gift.

Timothy and Titus made a beeline for a display of tomahawks—which were right next to a barrel of rubber snakes.

Sarah-Jane shuddered. Then she got down

to business. She had her own system for a shopping situation like this. First she had to do an overview of the whole store. See everything there was to see. Then she would get down to the hard work of deciding between a miniature pinto pony and a beaded coin purse.

Sarah-Jane barely glanced at the clothes as she sailed by. She didn't have money for Big Ticket items. But something had caught her eye. Slowly she walked back to look. What she saw made her catch her breath. . . .

It was like pulling teeth to drag Timothy and Titus away from the rubber snakes to get them to look at clothes.

But Sarah-Jane could do just about anything when she set her mind to it.

And this was important to her. It proved that she wasn't completely crazy.

"I'm telling you, S-J, this had better be good," growled Timothy.

"It had better be EX-cellent!" growled Titus.

It was.

The boys stood staring where Sarah-Jane pointed. And she could tell right away that they understood.

They were looking at a beautiful jacket. It had long, swingy fringes and fancy beaded decorations.

But that wasn't what fascinated the cousins.

What fascinated them was that they had seen a jacket just like this one in the woods that morning.

# 8

## Funny Weird

"**S**o you see what I mean," said Sarah-Jane. "What we saw was just an ordinary tourist with a long, dark braid and a fancy jacket. Definitely not the Indian Maiden. Probably not even an Indian person at all."

Glad as she was to have this logical explanation, Sarah-Jane couldn't help feeling a little disappointed about the jacket. It was the same way she had felt about the aluminum canoe. It was all so . . . so . . . *ordinary*.

Timothy and Titus seemed to understand how she was feeling. And they tried to cheer her up.

"OK," said Titus. "So what if she *was* just an ordinary tourist? Or maybe an ordinary person who lives here in town? That still doesn't explain what she was doing at that end of the lake. The island is closed for the season. Misty Pines is closed for the season. So what was she doing way down there?"

"Right," agreed Timothy. "We know she wasn't out for an ordinary boat ride, because she *landed*. And in a pretty sneaky way, remember."

Sarah-Jane suddenly felt a lot more cheerful. "You're right! It was sneaky, wasn't it? And you know what's funny?"

"Funny ha-ha? Or funny weird?" asked Titus.

"Funny weird," said Sarah-Jane.

"What's funny weird?" asked Timothy.

"The way the F.I.M. didn't stay long," replied Sarah-Jane.

But Timothy and Titus were staring at her blankly again. "The *F.I.M.*?" they said together.

"Fake Indian Maiden," said Sarah-Jane impatiently. "Please try to keep up. Now, where was I? Oh, yes. I was saying it's weird how the F.I.M.—"

"The *fim*," said Titus.

Now it was Sarah-Jane's turn to look blank. "The *what*?"

"The *fim*," repeated Titus. "F-I-M spells *fim*. So why not just call her that? Saves time."

"Saves Tim!" cried Timothy, sounding very pleased with this.

Sarah-Jane waited until he and Titus had stopped laughing.

"As I was saying—" began Sarah-Jane in her best Teacher-Voice. "It's funny weird how the *fim* didn't stay long in the woods. She goes to all the trouble to land and hide the canoe. But she didn't stay long at all. She was gone before we got back with my parents. Why? What was she doing?"

Titus had gotten over his giggles by then. He said, "You know, we were so thrown by the canoe being gone that we forgot to do something."

"We didn't even go look in the woods," said Timothy. "We didn't look around for clues."

Suddenly, spending hours in the souvenir shop didn't seem so important anymore.

The cousins hurried through their shopping. The plan was to grab a bite to eat and get back to Misty Pines as soon as possible.

But things don't always go according to plan.

# 9

## A Flash in the Sun

"You're all done shopping?" exclaimed Sarah-Jane's mother in surprise. "How did *that* happen? I thought you'd take forever. I've just started."

Mrs. Cooper had run into someone she hadn't seen in a long time, and they were catching up on all the news.

The chances of getting back to Misty Pines anytime soon did not look good.

Still, Sarah-Jane tried to move things along. "We're *hung-gree!*" she said in her best Weak-Little-Kitten-Voice. (By this time, the statement was perfectly true.)

Timothy and Titus slumped against the counter to show that they barely had the strength to stand up.

"You clowns!" said Mrs. Cooper cheerfully. "You were the ones who wanted to go shopping first and have lunch later, remember? Just give me a few minutes to finish up here."

The cousins knew when they were licked.

Somehow they managed to stumble outside and collapse on a bench in the sunshine.

"A few minutes," said Timothy. "How many do you suppose that is?"

"I don't think anyone can count that high," said Titus.

"I'm *hung-gree!*" wailed Sarah-Jane.

She leaned back and half closed her eyes. She was watching all the people who were admiring the lake.

Suddenly she sat up so quickly that Timothy and Titus jumped.

"Binoculars!" said Sarah-Jane.

"We don't have any binoculars," said Timothy.

"Not with us, anyway," said Titus.

"I don't mean the kind of binoculars you wear around your neck," said Sarah-Jane. "I mean the kind on a pole. The kind you put a quarter in. There's one right over here! Look!"

Whenever the cousins had to wait for any

of their parents, they were not allowed to wander off. Fortunately, the binoculars belonged to the Indian Trails souvenir shop. It was a new addition just this year.

"Let's see if we can see all the way to Misty Pines," said Sarah-Jane.

Timothy and Titus jumped up. They knew a good idea when they heard one.

Sarah-Jane got out a quarter and dropped it in the slot.

She got to go first since it was her idea. Not to mention her quarter.

It took a while to focus and get the binoculars aimed in the right direction. But when she did, the view was spectacular.

The mist of the morning had burned off, and the day was sparkling.

Through the binoculars Sarah-Jane saw dozens and dozens of gleaming white sea gulls. They were swooping in circles around one end of the island. There was something about that . . .

But Sarah-Jane didn't have time to think it through, because Timothy and Titus were calling "Time!"

Sarah-Jane waited impatiently for it to be

her turn again. What was it about the sea gulls? Then—at last!—it was her turn. She turned the binoculars back toward the island, looking for the gleaming white sea gulls against the blue, blue sky. Watching them swoop down to the—

Suddenly something else caught her eye. Something else was gleaming in the sun. Something silver.

Sarah-Jane gasped. "You guys! *Look!*"

But at that moment there was a little whir-ring noise followed by a click. Their time was up. The binoculars went blank.

# 10

## The Clue of the Sea Gulls

*F*rantically Timothy and Titus fumbled for change. (Sarah-Jane was all out.)

"Hurry! Hurry!" she cried.

But by the time one of them found a quarter and dropped it into the slot, it was too late.

"Oh!" said Sarah-Jane. "It's gone!"

"What's gone?" asked Titus, taking his turn. "What are we supposed to be looking for?"

"I saw a flash of silver," replied Sarah-Jane.

"You mean—like the *canoe*?" asked Timothy. "Where?"

He took his turn and began scanning the water.

"No," said Sarah-Jane, turning the binoculars in the direction of the island. "Look over there."

"But that's the island," said Titus.

"Exactly," said Sarah-Jane.

She found the spot where she had seen the canoe and turned the binoculars over to Titus.

"I still don't see it," said Titus.

"No, it's gone now," said Sarah-Jane. "But it was right there. On the shore. It was like someone had pulled it part of the way up on land. And then by the time I looked again, they had pulled it all the way up."

Timothy and Titus didn't say anything. They were wearing That Look again. It reminded Sarah-Jane of when she had first told them about the Indian Maiden.

"You don't believe me! Again!" she screeched.

"No—it's not that," said Titus. "It's just that—well, how could there be a boat on the island if there are no people there now?"

Somewhere in the back of her mind, Sarah-Jane knew she had the answer to that. She just needed a moment to think about it.

But just then a cheerful voice behind them said, "OK, you guys! Lunchtime at last!"

The cousins had been so involved with the binoculars that they had forgotten all about Sarah-Jane's mother. They had forgotten all about Sarah-Jane's mother's friend. They had forgotten all about the Indian Trails souvenir shop. They had even forgotten all about lunch.

"Mom!" wailed Sarah-Jane. "Do we have to eat *now*? We're busy!"

Sarah-Jane's mother shook her head in amazement as if to say, "What is with this child?"

And just then the binoculars whirred and clicked off.

"It looks as if you're at a good stopping point," said her mother. "You can come back after lunch if you want to."

Sarah-Jane didn't argue.

For one thing, her mother's friend was coming to lunch with them. And Sarah-Jane didn't want to look like a total brat in front of company.

For another thing, some other people were waiting to use the binoculars.

And for another thing, she was *HUNG-GREE!*

Oddly enough, it was thinking about being

hungry that suddenly made that other thing click into place. . . .

The ladies were walking ahead toward the restaurant.

Sarah-Jane was glad her mother hadn't asked what they'd been looking at through the binoculars. She was glad not to have to say, "Mom—you know that canoe you never saw? Well, it disappeared again. Except this time I know where it is. Only no one believes me."

No, it was better not to have to try to explain all that to her mother. However. Sarah-Jane most definitely *did* have something to say to her cousins. She stopped and turned around with her hands on her hips. "No one on the island, eh? Well, tell that to the sea gulls."

# 11

## *A Stranger on the Island*

$T$he restaurant was crowded. Sarah-Jane's mother and her friend gave their names to the hostess. The cousins stood off by themselves and talked about the mystery.

"OK, S-J," said Timothy, who didn't want to wait another minute for an explanation. "What's all this about sea gulls?"

"I *mean*," said Sarah-Jane. "That there were so many of them."

Timothy and Titus exchanged a puzzled glance.

Titus said, "Of course there were a lot of them. That's why it's called Gull Island."

But Sarah-Jane shook her head. "I mean there were so many of them *in one place*. Usually when you see sea gulls, it's one here, one there. They go off by themselves, looking for food. Just flying back and forth. But when you see *lots* and *lots* of them circling like a—a—" She paused and tried to come up with the right description. "Like a 'bird tornado,' then you know they've *found* food. And they've found it all in one place."

From the looks on her cousins' faces, Sarah-Jane could see the wheels turning.

"Meaning . . ." said Titus slowly.

"Meaning . . ." said Timothy.

"Meaning . . ." said Sarah-Jane, "that someone was on the island feeding them. Or it could be the gulls just found scraps from somebody's food."

"It's possible," admitted Timothy.

"Except—I thought no one was on the island now," said Titus.

"No one is *supposed* to be on the island now," corrected Sarah-Jane. "It's not the same thing."

"So what are you saying?" asked Timothy. "That someone *snuck* over there to feed the sea gulls?"

"Not just anyone," said Sarah-Jane. "It

was the *fim*—the Fake Indian Maiden. I saw her canoe, remember."

Timothy and Titus glanced at each other.

"That could have been an optical illusion, S-J," said Titus. "What with the sun shining on the water and all that."

Sarah-Jane shrugged. "Sure. It *could* have been. But it wasn't. It was the *fim*. And she didn't just go over there to feed sea gulls. She's over there for some other reason. And she's up to no good."

"*What* other reason?" asked Timothy and Titus together.

"I don't know," said Sarah-Jane, giving an airy little wave of her hand as their table was called. "I never jump to conclusions."

# 12

## Sarah-Jane's Mother's Friend

*T*he ladies were talking at the table.

The cousins were looking around for their food.

The waitress had taken their order only a few minutes ago. But, by this time, Timothy, Titus, and Sarah-Jane were ready to eat the silverware.

So they were not completely tuning in to the grown-ups' conversation.

But that didn't mean they were completely tuning out, either.

So they heard Sarah-Jane's mother say, "Paula, it has been such a treat running into you like this! I'm so glad I brought the kids to

town. Otherwise we would have been so close, but we would have missed each other—with you going out there tomorrow."

And they heard Sarah-Jane's mother's friend say, "Same here, Sue! I'm so glad I decided to come down a day early and spend it here in town. In comfort. When the others arrive tomorrow, I know they'll give me a hard time about it."

Paula laughed. "I'm always getting teased. You'd think someone in my line of work would enjoy 'roughing it.' But I don't! Come to think of it, I'm not that crazy about boats, either."

Sarah-Jane's mother couldn't help teasing. "Then, camping out on an island is perfect for you."

"Ugh!" said Paula. "The things I do for science."

Sarah-Jane's mother looked across at her daughter and nephews and said, "This will interest you kids. Dr. Duncan is one of the scientists who's going out to Gull Island."

Interest them! They were now staring at Dr. Duncan with their mouths hanging open.

Sarah-Jane made a mental note to pay more attention to her parents' friends. You never knew when they might turn out to be interesting.

"What kind of animals are you studying?" asked Titus.

Titus loved animals. He wanted to be a scientist himself someday.

But Dr. Duncan smiled and shook her head. "I'm not that kind of scientist," she told him.

"Oh," said Titus, sounding a little disappointed. But he perked up right away out of curiosity. "Then, what—?"

"I'm an archaeologist," she said.

"An archaeologist!" exclaimed Timothy. "That means you dig up old cities and stuff."

Dr. Duncan nodded. "That's a pretty good way of putting it. I dig up stuff."

"But what is there to dig up on the island?" asked Titus.

"Treasure," said Sarah-Jane dreamily. "Hidden long, long ago by the beautiful Indian Maiden."

Now it was Dr. Duncan's turn to stare. "How on earth did you know that?" she asked.

# 13

## *Treasure*

*S*arah-Jane had the good sense to keep her voice down. But the words still came out squeaky with excitement.

"You mean there really *is* a treasure?" she asked. "I was just talking about the Indian Maiden legend. It's one of my favorite stories. But I never thought there might *really* be a treasure. And if anyone would think that, it would be me. That's because I have an active imagination."

Dr. Duncan smiled at her. "The Indian Maiden legend is one of my favorite stories, too. In fact, that's the main reason I became an archaeologist. I love stories. I love learning about people who lived long ago."

She paused for a moment and went on

thoughtfully. "Whenever you hear a legend like the one of the Indian Maiden and the island—"

"The *Lost* Island, we call it," said Sarah-Jane.

"The Lost Island!" said Dr. Duncan. "Great name! Well, whenever you hear a story like that, you have to wonder if there's anything to it. How did it get started? Not that I expect to find an actual treasure of gold and jewels. But the simplest clay pot can be a treasure to a museum.

"It could be that there was once a settlement on the island. If so, we'd like to learn about it. Who were those people? How did they live? Where did they go?"

"Did people used to live there long ago?" asked Sarah-Jane.

"Well," replied Dr. Duncan, "recently, a visitor to the island found a wonderful piece of pottery and turned it over to us. We need to find out more. That's why the island was closed early this season. The archaeologists have to get out to the island and see what we have here. Naturally, we've been trying to keep it quiet. That's why I was so startled when

Sarah-Jane mentioned the Indian Maiden's treasure."

Timothy said, "It was honest of that person to hand over the pottery, wasn't it?"

"Yes, it was," agreed Dr. Duncan. "He knew that something found on restricted land like the island was not his to keep. And he also knew the pottery was important for research."

Titus said, "What if a *dis*honest person found the pottery?"

"That would be a different matter, wouldn't it?" said Dr. Duncan sadly. "He might keep it for himself. Or he might sell it for a lot of money. Some buyers are in the market for certain things. And they don't care where or how the seller has gotten them."

By this time the food had arrived. It was delicious. But Sarah-Jane hardly noticed what she was eating. She was thinking hard.

Dr. Duncan noticed and asked, "What's up, Sarah-Jane?"

"It's probably just my imagination," said Sarah-Jane with a worried frown.

"Imagination is a wonderful thing," said Dr. Duncan softly. "Scientists couldn't do their work without it. Yes, we have to test our ideas and try to find proof. But we couldn't even get started if we didn't have a hunch about something."

Seeing how seriously Dr. Duncan was taking her, Sarah-Jane said earnestly, "Then, I have a hunch. I know you don't like boats, Dr. Duncan. But I think you need to rent one right now. Today. If you wait till your team comes tomorrow, it might be too late."

# 14

## The T.C.D.C. on Board

*F*or once in her life, Sarah-Jane hoped that she was wrong.

Timothy and Titus helped her explain about seeing the Fake Indian Maiden and the canoe.

(The boys were now totally convinced that Sarah-Jane had seen the canoe on the island and that she had been right about the sea gulls.)

Dr. Duncan couldn't get over how observant the cousins were and how they had thought so much through.

"That's the T.C.D.C.," said Mrs. Cooper proudly.

"What's a 'teesy-deesy'?" asked Dr. Duncan.

"It's letters," explained Sarah-Jane. "Capital T. Capital C. Capital D. Capital C. It stands for the Three Cousins Detective Club."

"Then, I would like the T.C.D.C. on board with me," said Dr. Duncan.

Mrs. Cooper left the car in town to pick up later. And they all went to see Sam, who ran the ferryboat. He also had smaller boats for rent. And when he heard that they had to check out a hunch that the site might have been tampered with, he agreed immediately to take them over.

"Anything for my beautiful fairy princess!" he cried.

By this he meant Sarah-Jane. The story of her expecting a *fairy* boat was one of his all-time favorite stories. So of course, he and Sarah-Jane's mother had to tell it to Dr. Duncan.

Nervous as they all were about what they would find on the island, the story made them feel better.

Unfortunately, what they found on the island was not good.

"Someone has been here," said Dr. Duncan grimly. "Someone is in the process of cleaning out the whole site. Who knows how much has already been taken or where it is? Oh, this is a disaster!"

"Maybe not," said Sarah-Jane. "I have another hunch."

# 15

## *Digging Stuff Up*

*T*imothy and Titus understood right away what Sarah-Jane was talking about.

The three cousins stood on the shore of the Lost Island and looked across the water to Misty Pines Campground.

It was only a few hours ago that they had walked along the campground footpath and looked toward the Lost Island.

Titus said, "We never checked the woods over there."

"Nope," said Timothy. "We never did."

"Well, then, gentlemen," said Sarah-Jane. "May I suggest we get busy?"

---

Dr. Duncan hadn't expected to find gold

and jewels, so it came as quite a surprise when she did. Handwork so beautiful it took your breath away—made long, long ago by people no one remembered.

The cousins had never seen an archaeologist so excited. Well, they had never seen an archaeologist—period. But that soon changed. Soon, as Titus pointed out, there were archaeologists as far as the eye could see.

It had all started when Sam took the cousins and Mrs. Cooper and Dr. Duncan off the island and dropped them at Misty Pines. Then the cousins had led Dr. Duncan to the spot on the path where the Fake Indian Maiden had appeared and disappeared. They searched the nearby woods and found the treasure.

"But why bring it here?" asked Dr. Duncan. "Why Misty Pines?"

"A couple of reasons," said Titus. "The first is that it's close. She probably had to make several trips, and she didn't have much time before you guys came to the island. Misty Pines is much closer to the island than any other spot on the lake."

"And the other reason is just as important," said Timothy. "There's hardly anybody here. The campground is closed for repairs. So she had an empty island and an almost empty campground. She probably figured she could just stash the stuff at Misty Pines and come back for it later."

"Do you suppose she still thinks that?" asked Titus.

"Who knows?" replied Sarah-Jane. "But we did a good job of messing up her plans."

"Ain't that the truth!" exclaimed Timothy.

"Of course it is," said Sarah-Jane. "Would I lie?"

## The End

# Series for Young Readers*
# From Bethany House Publishers

★ ★ ★

## THE ADVENTURES OF CALLIE ANN
### by Shannon Mason Leppard

Readers will giggle their way through the true-to-life escapades of Callie Ann Davies and her many North Carolina friends.

★ ★ ★

## BACKPACK MYSTERIES
### by Mary Carpenter Reid

This excitement-filled mystery series follows the mishaps and adventures of Steff and Paulie Larson as they strive to help often-eccentric relatives crack their toughest cases.

★ ★ ★

## THE CUL-DE-SAC KIDS
### by Beverly Lewis

Each story in this lighthearted series features the hilarious antics and predicaments of nine endearing boys and girls who live on Blossom Hill Lane.

★ ★ ★

## RUBY SLIPPERS SCHOOL
### by Stacy Towle Morgan

Join the fun as home-schoolers Hope and Annie Brown visit fascinating countries and meet inspiring Christians from around the world!

★ ★ ★

## THREE COUSINS DETECTIVE CLUB®
### by Elspeth Campbell Murphy

Famous detective cousins Timothy, Titus, and Sarah-Jane learn compelling Scripture-based truths while finding—and solving—intriguing mysteries.

* (ages 7–10)